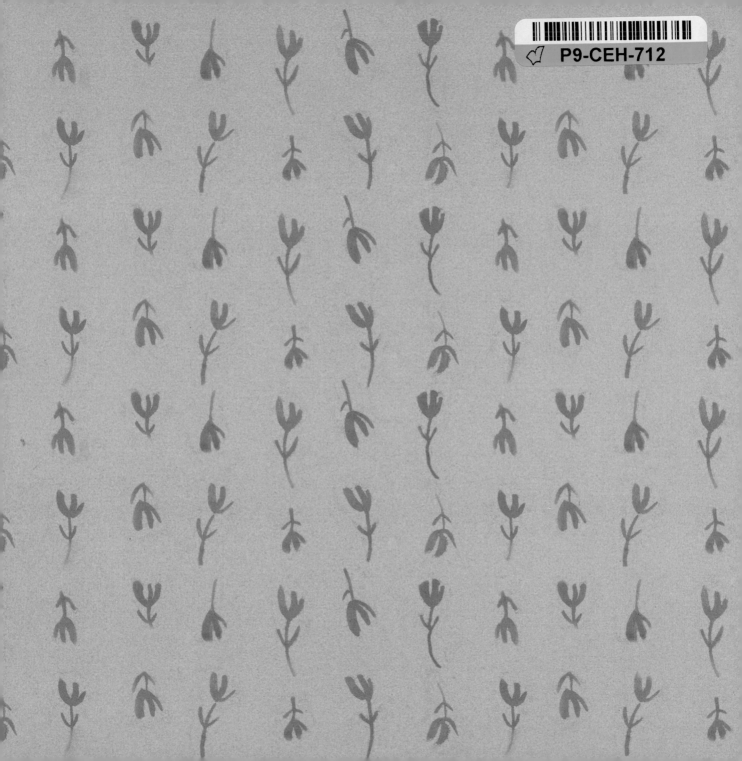

I Can Say Thank You

For my sister, Jocelyn ~ T.A.

First American Edition 2011
Kane Miller, A Division of EDC Publishing

Text and illustrations copyright © 2010 Tamsin Ainslie
First published in Australia by Little Hare Books
First published in the United States of America by Kane Miller in 2011
by arrangement with Australian Licensing Corporation

For information contact:
Kane Miller, A Division of EDC Publishing
P.O. Box 470663
Tulsa, OK 74147-0663
www.kanemiller.com
www.edcpub.com

Library of Congress Control Number: 2010941086

Printed through Phoenix Offset
Printed in Shen Zhen, Guangdong Province, China, April 2011
1 2 3 4 5 6 7 8 9 10
ISBN: 978-1-61067-038-8

I Can Say Thank You

Tamsin Ainslie

Kane Miller
A DIVISION OF EDC PUBLISHING

Come and play with me.

Thank you!

What clever cartwheels!

Thank you!

These flowers are for you.

Listen while I tell a story.

Thank you!

You can fly our kite.

Thank you!

You are good at
guessing cloud shapes.

Borrow our umbrella!

Thank you!

It is fun playing with you!

Warm your toes by my fire.

Thank you!

Thank you for a fun day!